CW00808851

I Can Achieve Anything

I can achieve ANYTHING

Written by MoNique Waters

Illustrated by Felicity LeFevre

I Can Achieve Anything
© 2021 by MoNique Waters

All rights reserved. No part of this publication may be reproduced in any form
or by any electronic or mechanical means, including information storage and
retrieval systems, without permission in writing by the publisher, except by a
reviewer who may quote brief passages in a review. For information regarding
permission, contact the publisher at books@daveburgessconsulting.com.

This book is available at special discounts when purchased in
quantity for educational purposes or for use as premiums, promotions,
or fundraisers. For inquiries and details, contact the publisher at
books@daveburgessconsulting.com.

Published by Dave Burgess Consulting, Inc.
San Diego, CA
DaveBurgessConsulting.com

Library of Congress Control Number: 2021946213
Hardcover ISBN: 978-1-956306-02-6
Paperback ISBN: 978-1-956306-01-9

Cover and interior design by Liz Schreiter
Illustrations by Felicity LeFevre
Editing and production by Reading List Editorial: readinglisteditorial.com

For my students and all of the beautiful people in this world.
Please never forget how special you are.
—MoNique

For Jameelah, Juwayriah, Sahlah, Asiyah, Hafsah, and Tameem.
You have all of the qualities in this book and so much more.
—Felicity

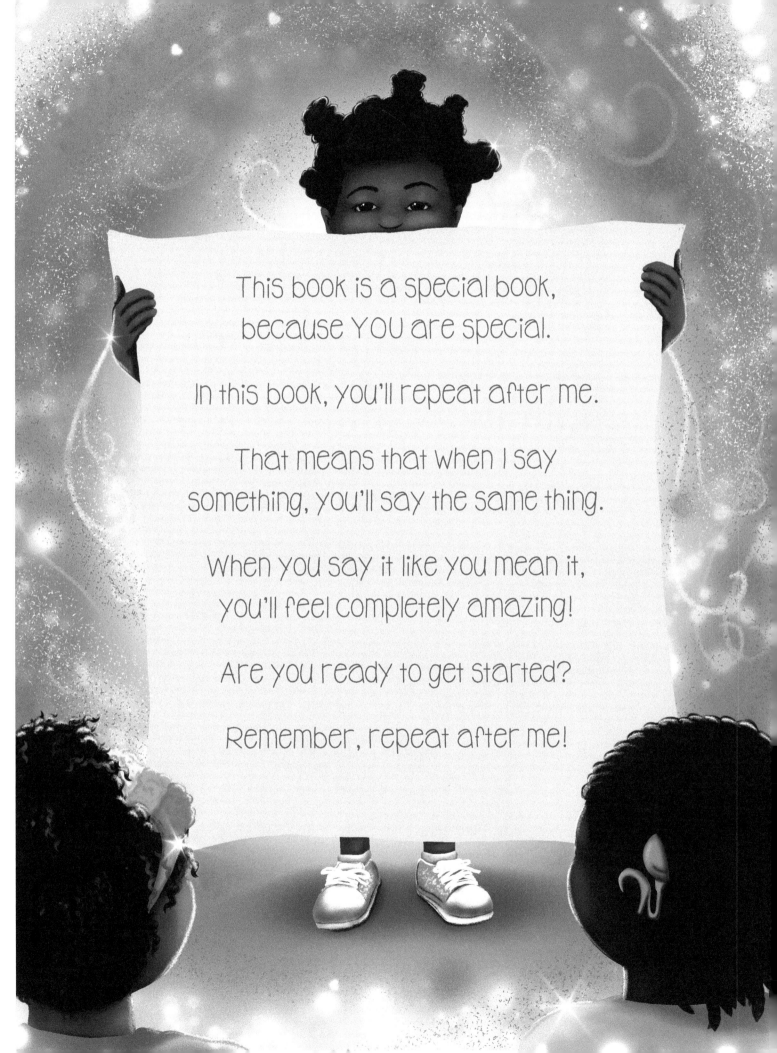

This book is a special book,
because YOU are special.

In this book, you'll repeat after me.

That means that when I say
something, you'll say the same thing.

When you say it like you mean it,
you'll feel completely amazing!

Are you ready to get started?

Remember, repeat after me!

I am Unique!

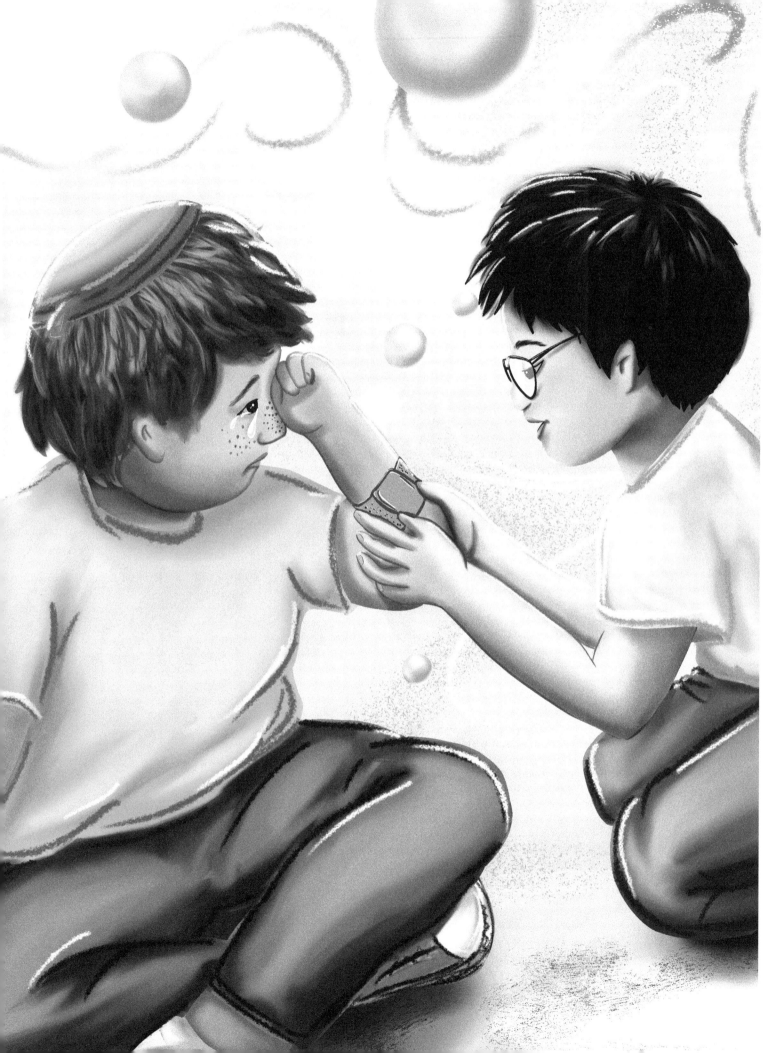

I am Confident!

Glossary

Baldness: There are many reasons a person may not have hair. Some people are born without hair or have a condition that makes their hair fall out. Sometimes certain medicines may cause someone's hair to fall out. Other people like the way they look without hair and choose to cut it off.

Cochlear Implant: A cochlear implant is a tool that helps someone who has trouble hearing. The part of the cochlear implant that you can see behind the ear has a microphone that picks up sound and helps a person hear.

Hijab: A hijab is a head covering worn by some Muslim women. There are many different styles and ways a hijab can be worn. When women or girls choose to wear a hijab, it shows respect and privacy.

Prosthetic Leg: A prosthetic leg is a leg that is made to replace a missing leg. Sometimes people are born without certain limbs, or they may lose an arm or leg in an accident, because of illness, or for another reason. A prosthetic limb is an option some people choose to use when this happens.

Vitiligo: Vitiligo is when a person has spots or patches of skin where color is missing. People with all different shades of skin can be born with vitiligo. It is not harmful to that person or other people.

Wheelchair: A wheelchair is a chair that has wheels on it. It can be used to help someone who has trouble walking or getting around. A person may have trouble walking because of illness, an accident, or a disability.

Yarmulke: A yarmulke is small cloth cap worn by Jewish men and boys. It is also called a kippah. It's usually worn during prayer or festivals, or for other events. The yarmulke is a symbol of respect for Judaism, the religion Jewish people practice.

About the Author

MoNique Waters has been an educator for over thirteen years, working with pre-K and primary students. She is passionate about creating spaces where all people feel seen, heard, and welcome. She devotes her time to teaching and learning from other educators around the world. *I Can Achieve Anything* is her first book and was inspired by her students. MoNique lives in Ohio with her family. You can find her online at Itsmoniquesworld.com and @itsmoniquesworld on Instagram.

About the Illustrator

Felicity LeFevre worked for eighteen years as a Pre-K and Kindergarten teacher, but she now devotes her time to social justice causes via her artwork, social media, and educational materials she creates. *I Can Achieve Anything* is the first children's book she's illustrated. Born and raised in New York City, she now lives in the South with her husband, Rashid, and the youngest three of her six children. You can find her on Instagram at @palettebyfelicity.

CPSIA information can be obtained
at www.ICGtesting.com
Printed in the USA
LVHW071630171221
706497LV00006B/103